The
NOISY NOSE
NANNY

ELAYNE REISS-WEIMANN

RITA FRIEDMAN

Published by

Arista Publishing
Two Park Avenue
New York, NY 10016

Printed in U.S.A.

ISBN 0-89796-986-3

2 3 4 5 6   SPC   8 9 8 7 6   12354

Mr. N is very excited.

He has a new job.

Mr. N is a birdsitter.

Nellie Nuthatch hires Mr. N to birdsit.

She shows Mr. N her sleeping babies.

"They cannot fly," says Nellie.

"Please be sure they do not fall out of the nest."

"Fly away, Nellie. Have a good time," says Mr. N.

"I will make sure your nuthatches stay in the nest.

Birdsitting is an easy job."

N

Mr. N sits under the tree.
His noisy nose is very noisy.
It awakens the nuthatches.
They hop to the edge of the nest.
"What's that noisy noise?" they ask,
stretching their necks.
Before Mr. N can answer, one nuthatch
starts to fall.

N

5

Mr. N runs beneath the nest.
He lifts up his head.
He catches the nuthatch.
It lands in his noisy nose.

Carefully, Mr. N places the nuthatch back
into the nest.
"It is fun to fall into your noisy nose," laughs
the nuthatch.
"May I do it again?"
"Let me try," shouts another nuthatch.
Before Mr. N can say a word, a second
nuthatch falls from the nest.
Quickly, Mr. N lifts up his head.
The nuthatch lands in his noisy nose.

N

The nuthatches line up on the edge of the nest.
"Catch us, Mr. N," they shout.
Poor Mr. N, he catches one nuthatch
after another.
He puts each one back into the nest.
But the nuthatches will not stay there.
"Birdsitting is not an easy job,"
sighs Mr. N.

At last Nellie Nuthatch returns.

"You are naughty nuthatches," she scolds.

"It is time you learn to fly."

Nellie tries to teach her nuthatches to fly.

But they will not learn.

"Oops, I am falling," says one nuthatch
after another.

Mr. N rushes to catch each one.

"Falling into a noisy nose is more fun than
learning to fly," laugh the nuthatches.

"They don't want to learn," sighs Nellie.

"What can I do?"

"I have an idea," smiles Mr. N, rushing away.

N

Mr. N returns in a few minutes, carrying
something behind his back.
He hears a baby nuthatch calling him.
"Mr. N, I am falling," laughs the nuthatch.
"Catch me! Catch me!"
Mr. N rushes to catch the nuthatch.
However, this time he does not use his
noisy nose.
He uses a net.

"A net does not make noise," says the
nuthatch unhappily.
"Catch me with your noisy nose."
"My noisy nose is not necessary anymore,"
says Mr. N.
"This net will catch you nicely."
Nellie continues to teach her nuthatches to fly.
Mr. N holds the net under them.
"It isn't any fun to fall into a net," say the
nuthatches.
Instead of falling, they learn to fly.

One day, it is too foggy for the baby
nuthatches to fly.
Nellie puts them to sleep in the nest.
She asks Mr. N to birdsit.
"My baby nuthatches will sleep all the time
I am gone," says Nellie.
"You will have an easy job."
As soon as Nellie flies away, the naughty
nuthatches fly out of the nest.
"Goodbye, Mr. N," they chirp.
"We'll be back before Mother returns."
Away they fly.

Mr. N waits and waits.

The nuthatches do not return.

Mr. N gets on his bicycle and tries to find them.

It is very foggy.

Mr. N. can hardly see.

"Maybe the nuthatches will hear my noisy nose,"
he thinks.

Suddenly, Mr. N hears voices calling his name.

Mr. N cannot see anyone.

"Look way up here," shout the voices.

Mr. N looks up.

It is difficult to see in the fog.

Finally, he sees the nuthatches at the top of a very tall tree.

"Please fly down," says Mr. N.

"We are afraid to fly down," cry the nuthatches.

"We can hardly see you."

"I will ride to town and get help," says Mr. N.

Mr. N. returns from town with helpers.
People hold a large safety net under the tree.
"Jump into this net. We will catch you," they
shout to the nuthatches.
"We will not jump," say the nuthatches.
"We can hardly see the net, and we do not
like landing in a net."
No one knows what to do.
Suddenly, Mr. N has an idea.

N

"Take the net away," says Mr. N.

"Listen!" he says to the nuthatches.

"What do you hear?"

"We hear your noisy nose," they answer.

"Do you like to fall into my noisy nose?"
asks Mr. N.

"Oh yes, it is great fun," laugh
the nuthatches.

"My noisy nose will catch each of you,"
says Mr. N.

"Who wants to jump first?"

The nuthatches forget they are afraid.
One by one, they jump.
It is not easy, but Mr. N catches each one
in his noisy nose.
Everyone cheers.
Mr. N puts the nuthatches into his
bicycle basket.
They fall asleep.
Mr. N rides back to the nest.
He places each sleeping nuthatch into
the nest.

29

Soon Nellie Nuthatch returns.

She finds her babies and Mr. N asleep.

"I guess no one has moved all day," says Nellie.